Star for a Day

Jean Ure

With illustrations by
Charlie Alder

Barrington Stoke

First published in 2020 in Great Britain by
Barrington Stoke Ltd
18 Walker Street, Edinburgh, EH3 7LP

www.barringtonstoke.co.uk

This 4u2read edition based on *Star for a Day*
(Barrington Stoke, 2014)

Text © 2020 Jean Ure
Illustrations © 2014 & 2020 Charlie Alder

A CIP catalogue record for this book is available
from the British Library upon request

ISBN: 978-1-78112-933-3

Printed in China by Leo

Contents

Chapter 1
Curtain Up

"Please, Mum," Lola cried. *"Please!"* She stamped her foot. "It's so not fair!"

Lola was in one of her sulks. She always sulks if she can't get her own way. She is my sister. My *little* sister. She is very spoilt.

I am Lucy, and I am not spoilt at all. Lola is two years younger than me and she is much prettier. Lola's hair is blonde and bubbly, mine is straight and the colour of mud. Lola is Mum's favourite. Mum calls her "my little princess". She calls me "Loopy Loo", or sometimes just Loopy.

I don't mind that much. I've got used to it. But Loopy Loo is a really stupid name unless you're about five. Grandad calls me "Luce", and I like that much better. Grandad lives with us. It's just him and Mum, and me and Lola. I get on really well with Grandad.

But back to Lola and her sulks. She was bright red by now, like a tomato. Her lips were wobbling, her eyes filling with tears. She is very good at crying.

"Mum?" she whispered, all pathetic.

I could see that Mum was starting to give in.

A girl called Holly had invited me and Lola to her birthday party. She was going to be 13, the same age as me. The party was on Saturday and Lola was desperate for Mum to take her into town, like STRAIGHT AWAY, to buy her something new to wear.

"I need something, Mum! It's a *party*," Lola cried.

"Well ... I don't know," Mum said. "I suppose, maybe ..."

Lola gave me a sly glance. She can always tell when she is about to get her own way.

"Holly will be all dressed up," she said. "She always is!"

"It's her party," Grandad said. "When it's your party, you can be the one to dress up."

Sometimes Grandad gets a bit sharp with Lola. Most of the time, Lola takes no notice of him. After all, what does Grandad know?

"If I can't have a new outfit," she said, "then I won't go!"

Grandad tutted.

"I mean it!" Lola screamed. "I won't go! She can, if she likes." *She* meant me, of course. "I'll just stay home!"

Lola always makes a lot of fuss, but it's important to her to look good. Some people like to be clever and pass exams. Some people like to be good at sport. Lola likes to wear pretty clothes.

Mum agrees that it's important to always look your best. And Lola knows just how to get round her.

"*Please*, Mum!" The tears were starting to roll down Lola's cheeks. She clasped her hands together. "Pretty please!"

Mum can never resist Lola's tears for very long. "Oh, all right," she said. "Let's go shopping!"

Chapter 2
Take Your Partner

"Hang about!" Grandad said. "What about Lucy? What's she going to wear to this party?"

Mum and Lola were already halfway out of the door. They stopped. Mum looked at Grandad with a frown.

"Lucy?" she said. Like, *why should Lucy need anything?*

"Your sister needs something for the party too," said Grandad.

Lola pouted. "Why?"

She is the one that has to look pretty! Not me.

Grandad gave Lola one of his looks. He would never say so, but I think he agrees with me ... Lola is spoilt rotten.

"The problem is," Mum said, "I can't afford to buy new clothes for both of them. Money doesn't grow on trees."

"No, and I got in first," said Lola.

Grandad shook his head. "Luce! Come here," he said softly.

I went over to him.

"Here," said Grandad. He slipped something into my hand. A £20 note! "Take this," he said. "Buy something nice. See what you can find."

"Grandad, thank you!" I threw my arms round Grandad's neck and kissed him.

I was so grateful to Grandad for giving me that money. I found a really cute top, which even Lola agreed was cool. Not *totally* cool. She was the only one that was *totally* cool. But now I felt good about myself, which I don't always do and never if I have to go anywhere with Lola. Parties are the worst.

Lola really sparkles at parties. She squeals a lot, and giggles a lot, and does all these little showing-off twirls, like, "Look at me, look at me!" And everybody does.

So there we were at Holly's place, me in my new cool top and Lola doing her thing. I was standing in a corner, watching her squeal and twirl, when this boy came up to me.

"Hi! I'm Tyler," he said. "Holly's cousin."

I felt myself blushing. Blushing is *so* embarrassing! Why do I have to blush all the time? Why blush just because a boy starts talking to you?

"Hi," I said. I was holding a glass of orange juice. I put it up to my face and mumbled. "I'm Lucy ... Lola's sister."

"Oh!" Tyler sounded surprised. I saw his eyes flicker across to Lola. "That's your sister?" I guessed he couldn't believe it. How could a girl that couldn't talk to a boy without going bright red have a sister as pretty and popular as Lola?

We stood there in silence and watched as Lola twirled. Tyler couldn't take his eyes off her.

Tyler turned, at last, to look at me. "How do you—" he began, and then broke off.

"How do I what?" I said.

"Well ..." He looked a bit awkward. "I don't mean to be rude. I was just going to say, how do you ... I mean ..." He was starting to go a bit red himself. "It can't be easy, having a sister like that."

I knew what he meant. It isn't always easy, having a sister who is so pretty and popular. I don't always like it very much. But before I could say anything, Lola came skipping over.

"Hey, Tyler!" she cried. She grabbed him by the hand. "Come and dance!"

She dragged him off across the room. I was left on my own with my glass of orange juice.

At least I had my nice new top. That was something.

Chapter 3
Star Quality

It was a week after the party and Lola was making a fuss again. It was about shoes, this time. *New* shoes. She was going for an audition and she absolutely had to have some.

"Mum, I need them," cried Lola. "How can I wear these horrible old things? Please, Mum! You've got to buy me some new ones."

Grandad gave me a look. I knew that we were both thinking the same thing. *Here we go again.*

"What's this audition for, anyway?" Grandad asked.

"It's for *Spotlight on Kids*," Mum said. "The talent show – on television."

She said it like Grandad should have known, but why should he? What did Grandad know about talent shows? Mum gets a bit cross with Grandad sometimes. He came to live with us a few months ago, after Gran had died. He was so lonely on his own. I didn't mind one bit when I had to move in with Lola and let him have my bedroom. Lola grumbled, but I was just glad that Grandad wasn't on his own any more.

"Last year," Mum said, "we got through to the second round. We were Highly Commended. Weren't we?" She smiled proudly at Lola.

"This year," said Lola, "I'm going to get to the finals. *If* I have some new ballet shoes!"

"Oh, we'll get them for you," said Mum.
"Don't worry. Let's see how much there is in
the savings pot."

The savings pot is an old cracked jug where
Mum puts her change. She and Lola rushed off
to the kitchen to count what was in there.

"I can't help thinking," Grandad said, "just
why are these new shoes so important?"

I told him how dance means everything to Lola.

"Oh, I know that," Grandad said. "But when your mum is so broke ... does Lola *really* have to have new shoes?"

"It's just for the audition," I said. "She does so want to get to the finals and be on television."

All Grandad said was, "Hm."

"She was really upset last year," I said, "when she only got Highly Commended."

I don't know why I always stick up for Lola. But she does work hard. *Really* hard. She is very serious about her dancing. I admire her for that. Even though she is a total pain.

"How about you?" Grandad said. "Why aren't you going in for it?"

"Me?" I said. "I can't dance!"

"Who says you can't?" said Grandad.

"Lola," I said. She says I'm like a stick insect. Mum says I'm like a matchstick. It's true, I'm a bit on the skinny side. Mum and Lola think it's very funny when I try to dance.

Grandad was frowning. "I know everyone thinks your sister is talented," he said.

"She is!" I told Grandad. "Her dance teacher says she has star quality."

"That may well be so," Grandad said. "But don't you ever think that you might have some talent of your own too?"

"Me?" I said.

It's true I do a lot better at school than Lola, but that doesn't mean I am *talented*. Just better at lessons.

"Do you remember," said Grandad, "that dance your gran taught you? The one you used to do for us when you were little?"

"Oh," I said. "The clog dance!"

Gran had been a champion clog dancer in her day. She had won medals. She'd tried to teach Lola, but Lola was never interested. She said clog dancing wasn't *real* dancing. Not like ballet.

"You were brilliant at it," Grandad told me. "Your gran always said you might have been a champion."

Gran had said that? About *me*?

"I'll tell you what," said Grandad. "I've still got your gran's old dancing shoes upstairs. Suppose I go and dig them out and we'll see how much you remember?"

Chapter 4
Let the Dance Begin

Lots of people think that you wear clogs to do clog dancing. Big, clumpy wooden clogs. But you don't. You wear normal shoes. Just shoes with metal bits on the bottom to make a good sound.

Gran's clog-dancing shoes were red lace-ups. They looked almost brand new. Grandad said in a sad voice that Gran hadn't worn them very often.

"Try them on," Grandad said. "See if they fit."

I didn't think there was very much chance, but, oh, they were perfect!

"I thought they'd be all right," Grandad said. "Your gran was like a little sparrow."

As soon as I'd got those red shoes on I wanted to start dancing. But where could I do it?

"Well, let's have a think," said Grandad. "We don't want your mum and sister to know what we're up to, do we? Best to keep it to ourselves, eh? Just you and me."

I nodded. The last thing I wanted was Lola to find out!

"I know where we'll go," Grandad said. "Come on!"

Grandad and I crept on tiptoe down the hall and out into the garden.

"Oh," I said. "The garage!"

Once upon a time the garage had had a car in it, but we didn't have a car any more. Mum said we couldn't afford to run it – not with all the money she had to spend on Lola's ballet classes. So now the garage was just an empty space. It was perfect.

"Right," said Grandad. "Let's see how much you remember."

My head didn't remember anything at all. But my feet did! They seemed to have a life of their own. As soon as they started to move, I knew exactly what to do.

As I danced, Grandad called out to me, just like Gran used to. "Step, step ... *down*. Watch that leg! Don't swing it back ... That's it, that's it, now you've got it!"

Once I had started, I didn't want to stop.
Gran had taught me lots of different dances. I
could have gone on all day!

Grandad said, "There, you see? A natural. Now we must decide which dance you're going to do."

"*Do?*" I said.

"For the talent show," Grandad said. "You are going to enter, aren't you?"

I stared at him.

"Come on," said Grandad. "You're a great little dancer."

But I was a stick insect! And Mum and Lola always laughed. How could I go in for a talent show and do clog dancing? *Clogging*, as Gran used to call it. Clogging wasn't proper dancing. Lola said it wasn't. And she was the expert.

"Trust me," Grandad said. "I didn't live with your gran all those years without learning a thing or two. You've got what it takes, girl! Be brave. Let's give it a go."

I'm not really a very brave sort of person, but I'd loved Gran, and I loved Grandad. I bit my lip. I guess Grandad could see that all I needed was a little push.

"Know what?" he said. "Your gran would be so proud of you. She always said you had the gift."

"Gran said that?"

Grandad nodded. "One of the best little clog dancers around."

I felt myself blush. Like I always do.

"So how about it?" said Grandad. "How do we apply for an audition?"

I took a deep breath. "Lola did it online," I said.

"Right," said Grandad. "Let's do it!"

We had to wait till Mum and Lola went into town to do some more shopping. (This time, it was to buy Lola a pink top to wear for her audition.) As soon as they left the house, Grandad and I sat down at the computer.

I typed in "Spotlight on Kids" and clicked on "Registration". A form came up and Grandad and I filled it in.

"Now what?" said Grandad.

"Look!" I pointed at the screen.

"Thank you," it read, "for registering with *Spotlight on Kids*. You will receive a letter in a day or two telling you where and when your audition will take place."

"What happens after that?" said Grandad. "You do the audition and then what?"

I told him that if you got through the first round, you went on to the second. And the winner of the second round went through to the finals – on television!

"Well, now," Grandad said. "That would be something, wouldn't it?"

Chapter 5
Break a Leg

My letter arrived two days later. It came flying through the door just as I was about to leave for school. I saw that it was addressed to "Miss L. French", so I snatched it up before Mum or Lola appeared. Nothing ever comes for me in the post apart from Christmas and birthday cards, but it wasn't Christmas and it wasn't my birthday, so I knew it had to be from *Spotlight on Kids*.

Lola came into the hall in time to see me stuff the letter into my bag. Lola has very sharp eyes. They miss nothing.

"What was that?" she said as we walked up to the bus stop together.

"What was what?" I said.

"You put something in your bag!" Lola narrowed her eyes. "Was it a letter?"

"When do I ever get letters?" I said.

"Dunno," said Lola. "But that's what it looked like."

"Apples look like peaches," I said. "It doesn't mean they are peaches."

I thought that was a really smart answer. At any rate, it made Lola think. It was several seconds before she said, "That's stupid! Apples don't look a bit like peaches."

"They do so," I said.

We argued about it all the way to the bus stop. At least it made her forget about the letter.

One of Lola's friends was on the bus.
"Hattie!" Lola squealed, and she rushed off
to sit with her.

Lola and Hattie sat at the front of the
bus; I sat at the back, where Lola couldn't see
me. With a hand that was a bit trembly, I slit
open the envelope and pulled out the letter. I
couldn't help giving a little squeak when I saw
what it said.

Dear Lucy

<u>*Spotlight on Kids*</u>
We are pleased to inform you that your audition will be held at 3 p.m. on Saturday, 6th July at the Cornflower Studios in Flower Street, Covent Garden. It should last no longer than five minutes. We look forward to seeing you.

Yours sincerely
Donna White
Spotlight on Kids

P.S. Please make sure to arrive on time.

My heart started to thump as I read it. What was I letting myself in for?

"When is your audition?" I asked Lola as we got off the bus.

"The 6th of July," she said.

"Is it in the morning," I said, "or the afternoon?"

She stared at me. "In the morning," she said.

At least we weren't both going to turn up at the same time. That was a relief.

Hattie linked her arm through Lola's. "What are you doing for the audition? Are you doing some ballet?" she asked.

"Yes." Lola gave a little skip and a hop. "Mum's making me a special outfit. I'm going to have a pink tutu and pink tights to go with my new pink shoes. And I've got a sparkly pink top as well."

Hattie looked at her admiringly. "Everything pink," she said.

"Yes," said Lola, "cos I'm the Sugar Plum Fairy!"

When I got home that afternoon, I showed Grandad my letter.

"Good," said Grandad. "Now we're really on our way."

I was still worried about what I was going to wear. I sat and watched as Lola showed off in front of us, skipping about in her new outfit, all pink and sparkly.

"Look at her!" said Mum. "Doesn't she look like a proper ballerina?"

Grandad and I agreed that she did. I wasn't jealous – I really wasn't. But there was just a little bit of me that wished I looked like a ballerina, too.

"What am I going to wear?" I asked Grandad later.

"Don't panic," said Grandad. "Let's see what your gran used to wear." He fetched down one of his photo albums and we looked at it together. "Anything take your fancy?" he asked.

"That's a nice one," I said. I pointed at a photo of Gran that I remembered from when I was little.

"Ah, yes," said Grandad. "That was at a festival. Your gran got properly dressed up for that one."

But she wasn't dressed up like a ballerina.
She just had a swirly skirt and a sparkly top. I
had a skirt a bit like that – and maybe I could
wear the new top I'd bought for Holly's party.

Next day, when Lola was out at her ballet
class, I stood in front of the mirror in our
bedroom and tried out my skirt and top with
Gran's clogging shoes. While I was studying
myself, Mum came in to put some clothes away.

"Oh!" she said. "That's a pretty top. Is that the one Grandad bought you?"

Mum had seen it before, when I'd worn it for the party. But sometimes she doesn't remember these things.

"It suits you," she said. "Blue's a good colour for you. You should wear it more often."

I glowed. If Mum said blue was a good colour, then I knew it had to be. Both Mum and Lola are really into clothes.

*

On the day of the auditions, Mum and Lola left the house at ten o'clock.

"Isn't anyone going to say break a leg?" Lola said.

I know that in the theatre "break a leg" means "good luck", but I think it's a bit odd. Why would anyone want to break a leg? Still, I said it for her, and so did Grandad.

Lola and Mum came home at lunch-time, very full of themselves.

"Honestly," said Mum, "some of the other acts were pathetic. One boy was playing the spoons, for goodness' sake!"

"And there was this girl," said Lola, "doing *street* dancing."

It seemed that street dancing was as bad as clogging. *Not real dance.* I began to wish I'd never listened to Grandad. Already I could feel my legs starting to wobble. By the time we arrived at Cornflower Studios that afternoon, they had almost turned to jelly.

"Grandad!" I grabbed at his sleeve. "I want to go home!"

Grandad took my hand and squeezed it. "Don't you worry," he said. "You'll be fine! Think of your gran – how happy she'd be. You can do it, Luce. Gran's the one you're dancing for. She'll be watching over you. You just get out there and do your stuff. All right?"

I nodded. I could be brave for Gran.

"Off you go," Grandad said. "I'll wait here for you. And, Luce ... break a leg!"

Chapter 6
Spotlight on Kids

I had to wait in a little side room until it was my turn to be called. Two other girls were in there. They were both older than me and obviously knew each other. They seemed very sure of themselves. As I came in, they stopped talking and turned to look at me. They watched while I took Gran's shoes out of my bag and put them on.

"Tap dancer, are you?" one asked.

"Clogger," I said.

"Clogger?" They both stared at me. "What's a clogger?"

"Clog dancing," I said.

"Oh," said the first one. She looked at the other and gave this smug nod. "Like tap for babies."

It so was *not*! But I wasn't going to argue. I was nervous enough before. By now I was almost frozen with terror. What was I doing here, with these two snooty girls?

At last it came to my turn. By now my legs really were like jelly. Three people were sitting at one end of the room, behind a table. A man and two women.

The man said, "Hello – Lucy, isn't it? Could you get up on stage for us?"

I wobbled up there.

One of the women gave me a kind smile. "Just start when you're ready," she said.

I wouldn't ever be ready! I wanted to go home. How could I dance when my legs were like jelly?

For a moment, I just stood there unable to move and then, all of a sudden, without any help from me, my feet just took over. Step, step – *down*. Step, step – *down*. My feet knew exactly what they were doing!

When I had finished, one of the women said, "Thank you very much, Lucy. You'll hear from us in a day or two."

I rushed out in a whirl to find Grandad. I was grinning from ear to ear.

"Grandad, I did it!" I yelled.

"Of course you did," said Grandad. "I knew you would. Was your old grandad right, or wasn't he?"

I hugged him and told him that he was.

"Really enjoyed yourself, didn't you?" said Grandad.

I had enjoyed myself so much I almost began to hope that I might have got through to the next round. I kept telling myself I was just being silly, but a few days later, when a letter arrived for Lola and nothing arrived for me, I felt sick and shaky.

"Mum, Mum," screeched Lola. "I've made it! I'm in the next round!"

"How could you not be?" said Mum. "My little princess! Well done!"

Mum clapped and so did I. But suddenly Lola let out a scream.

"*M-U-U-U-U-M!*"

"What?" said Mum. "What's the matter?"

Lola pushed the letter over to her. Mum took one look and turned pale.

"*Dear LUCY?*" She grabbed the envelope. "It's addressed to Miss L. French"

"Me," screamed Lola. "*Me!*"

"They must have made a mistake," said Mum. "But how did they get Lucy's name?"

Grandad had picked up the pile of post that Lola had dumped on the table. Most of it looked like boring stuff. Bills and brown envelopes. Brown envelopes are always boring. But right at the bottom was another white one.

"Miss L. French?" said Grandad.

"Let me see that!" Mum tore it away from him. She ripped it open. "*Dear Lola* ... this is the one."

"So what's the other one?" cried Lola. "What are they writing to her for?"

"It must be some kind of mix-up," said Mum.

"I don't think so," Grandad said. "Looks to me like you've got two daughters in the next round."

"How can she be in it?" shouted Lola. "She didn't even do an audition!"

"Want to bet?" said Grandad. He gave me a wink.

"When did she do one?" Mum sounded put out. She looked at me crossly. "How could you do an audition without me knowing?"

"And what could she do?" Lola said. "She can't dance! She can't sing!"

Grandad gave me a cheeky look. "Shall we tell them?" he asked.

Of course, we had to.

Lola said, "Clogging? That's not proper dancing!"

"It seems the judges thought it was," said Mum. "Oh, my goodness ... both of you in the next round." She beamed. "What talented daughters I have!"

Mum was so excited she rang the local paper and that very same day they sent a reporter. On Friday there was a big photo of me and Lola with the headline:

SISTERS STAR IN TALENT SHOW!

I expect Lola would rather have had her picture in the paper all by herself, but she got to dress up as the Sugar Plum Fairy in her pink tutu and her pink tights, so that made her happy. Mum was proud as could be.

"Who would have thought it?" she said.

"I would," said Grandad. "Well, I did," he said. "I did think it!"

Chapter 7
You Rock!

On my way home from school on Monday, I bumped into Tyler. I hadn't seen him since Holly's party. All at once I felt silly and shy and wanted to hide. But there wasn't anywhere *to* hide. Not unless I dived into someone's garden and crouched behind a hedge, and even I'm not that pathetic.

"Hi," Tyler said.

"Hi," I mumbled.

I was already starting to turn pink. But Tyler looked embarrassed too. I was so glad it wasn't just me.

"I saw your picture in the paper," he said. "I didn't know you could dance."

"Only clogging," I said. "My gran taught me when I was little."

"You must be very good at it."

I made a gurgling sound.

"So when's the next round?" Tyler asked.

"Next week," I said. "But I won't win."

"How do you know?" said Tyler.

"Cos Lola will," I said.

"Your sister." He seemed a bit awkward as he said it. It probably meant he had a crush on her. Lots of boys do. And then he said, "I'm really sorry about ... you know. At the party. What I said."

It can't be easy, having a sister like that. That was what he had said.

"I know she's popular, but ..." Tyler shifted from one foot to the other. "She is a bit of a show-off, isn't she?"

Oh! Did that mean he *didn't* have a crush on her?

"I'm just not sure how you put up with it," he muttered.

"I'm kind of used to it by now," I said. "I don't really notice any more."

That wasn't totally true, cos you can't help noticing. But I didn't want Tyler to think I was jealous or anything.

"I don't suppose," he said, "that you'd like to—"

His words were cut short by a sudden cry of, "Hey, Tyler!" It was Lola. "What are you doing here?" she said.

"Just on my way home," said Tyler. "Gotta go!"

We watched as he raced across the road and vanished up Oak Avenue.

"What were you talking to him about?" said Lola.

"Just things," I said.

"What things?"

Lola sounded really put out. She's not used to boys talking to me. But I was put out, too. What had Tyler been going to say? *I don't suppose you'd like to …* what? Thanks to my dear little sister, I would never know. I began to ask myself how I *did* put up with her.

Next day, an envelope fell on to the front door mat. Lola rushed to pick it up. And then she pouted and said, "Oh." She tossed it on to the hall table. "It's for you," she said.

I picked it up. It was addressed to "Miss Lucy French". Inside was a card. It was from Tyler! On the front was a picture of clogs. His handwriting was very neat and careful.

Hi Lucy

You rock! I don't suppose you would like to go out with me some time? Let me know. Give me a call.

Hope to see you soon.
Tyler

And then at the bottom he had written his phone number. I had never had a boy's phone number before!

"Who's that from?" said Lola.

"None of your business," I said.

"Oh! Well, if that's the way you feel." She tossed her head. "See if I care!"

Lola ran off down the hall. "Mu-u-um," she cried. "Lucy's got all big headed just cos she's in the next round!"

Chapter 8
Stars Always

Now I had a secret! But I wasn't telling! Not just yet.

The day of the second round arrived. The auditions were being held in the same place as before, the Cornflower Studios, only this time there was an audience ...

Twenty of us were taking part. The boy who played the spoons was there, and the girl who did street dancing. Much to Mum and Lola's disgust!

I did have a few butterflies when it was my turn to go on stage, but as soon as I started to dance, I was fine. I just pretended that I was back in Gran's kitchen, dancing for her

and Grandad. And guess what? I got Highly Commended! Same as Lola got last year.

Grandad hugged me and said, "Your gran would be so proud of you."

Even Mum cried, "Well done!" and gave me a kiss.

Lola won first place. She had got through to the finals. She was going to be on television! I truly thought she deserved it. She had worked so hard for so long. I clapped as hard as anybody when she went up for her prize.

As soon as we got home, Mum went to the fridge and took out a special bottle of sparkly drink, which she had put in there "just in case". Lola and I both had a glass, and Mum and Grandad drank a toast to us.

"To our two little stars!"

"Only for the day," said Lola.

"Oh, come on!" said Mum. "What are you talking about? *Only for the day?*"

"Being a star doesn't last for ever," said Lola. She gave me this look. "If you want to keep on being a star, you have to work at it."

"Oh, well. Yes, of course," Mum said. "I can't argue with that." And then she turned to me and said, "Does this mean you'll want to start dancing classes as well?"

Lola scowled. She didn't like that idea! But I told Mum that I wouldn't want to be a dancer.

"As a matter of fact," I said, "I think I'd like to be a doctor."

It was the first time I'd ever told anyone. I'd always had this feeling that Mum might laugh. *You?* she would go. *A doctor?* But she didn't.

Mum just said, "Oh!" She sounded a bit surprised. "Well, that would be brilliant. But you're still a star, even if it is only for a day. Let's make it two days ... let's all go up the road for a pizza tomorrow and have a proper celebration. How about that?"

The time had come to tell my secret.

"I can't tomorrow," I said.

They all turned to stare at me.

"Why's that?" said Mum.

I took a deep breath. "Cos I'm going out with Tyler," I said.

"Tyler?" Lola's eyes almost popped out of her head. "You've got a date with *Tyler*?"

"Why shouldn't she have?" said Mum. "No problem. We can go on Sunday."

"She won't still be a star by then," said Lola.

"Oh, I think she will," said Mum. "You both will!" And she put one arm round me and one arm round Lola, "You'll always be stars for me. Both of you."